Gargoylz

Take a Trip

Gargoylz: grotesque stone
creatures found on old
buildings, spouting rainwater
from the guttering.
Sometimes seen causing
mischief and mayhem
before scampering away
over rooftops.

www.kidsatrandomhouse.co.uk

Gargoylz

Take a Trip

Burchett & Vogler

illustrated by Leighton Noyes

RED FOX

GARGOYLZ TAKE A TRIP

A RED FOX BOOK 978 1 862 30867 1

First published in Great Britain by Red Fox,
an imprint of Random House Children's Books
A Random House Group Company

This edition published 2009

1 3 5 7 9 10 8 6 4 2

Series created and developed by Amber Caravéo
Copyright © Random House Children's Books, 2009

The Random House Group Limited supports the Forest Stewardship
Council (FSC), the leading international forest certification organization.
All our titles that are printed on Greenpeace-approved FSC-certified paper
carry the FSC logo. Our paper procurement policy can be found at
www.rbooks.co.uk/environment

Set in Bembo Schoolbook

Red Fox Books are published by Random House Children's Books,
61–63 Uxbridge Road, London W5 5SA

www.kidsatrandomhouse.co.uk
www.rbooks.co.uk

Addresses for companies within The Random House Group Limited can be
found at: www.randomhouse.co.uk/offices.htm

THE RANDOM HOUSE GROUP Limited Reg. No. 954009

A CIP catalogue record for this book is available from the British Library.

Printed in the UK by CPI Bookmarque, Croydon CR0 4TD

For Jacqui and Alan, with love
– **Burchett & Vogler**

To Amy.P
– **Leighton Noyes**

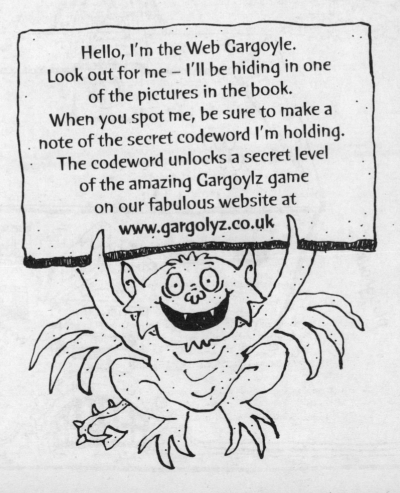

Hello, I'm the Web Gargoyle.
Look out for me – I'll be hiding in one
of the pictures in the book.
When you spot me, be sure to make a
note of the secret codeword I'm holding.
The codeword unlocks a secret level
of the amazing Gargoylz game
on our fabulous website at
www.gargolyz.co.uk

Oldacre Primary School

garden

staff car park

staffroom

playing field

playground

St Mark's Church

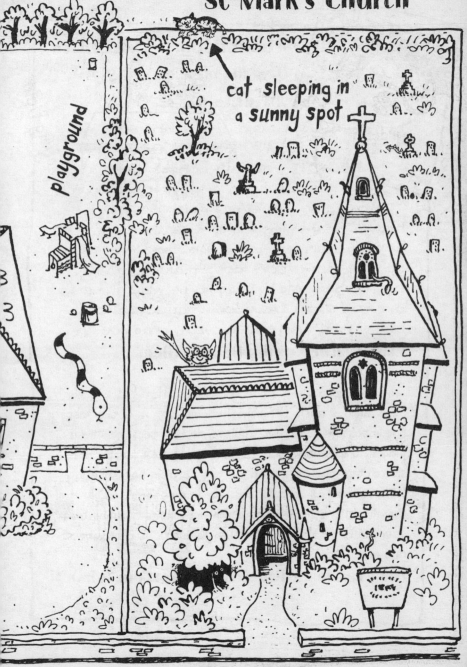

cat sleeping in a sunny spot

playground

School Report - Max Black

Days absent: 0

Days late: 0

Max is a bright boy. If he spent as much time on his school work as he does on annoying Lucinda Tellingly he would get much better marks. I am pleased to see that he enjoys exercise - although I do not count running down corridors making racing car noises. Also I would be glad if he did not shout "Awesome" quite so loudly every time we have football practice.

Class teacher - Miss Deirdre Bleet

The only good thing I can say about Max Black is that he is always early for school. However, he is the last one into the classroom. He spends far too much time playing tricks with Ben Neal. Mrs Pumpkin is still off sick after discovering an earwig farm in her handbag. Max ignores all school rules. He has recently developed a curious interest in drainpipes and has been seen talking to the wall. This behaviour is outrageous and must stop.

Head teacher - Hagatha Hogsbottom (Mrs)

School Report - Ben Neal

Days absent: 0

Days late: 0

Ben has many abilities which he does not always use. He works very hard at dreaming up tricks to play, which gives him very little time to concentrate on his learning. He enjoys football and skateboarding - indeed, he and his board can frequently be found upside down in a flowerbed.

Class teacher - Miss Deirdre Bleet

Ben Neal is a strange boy. He is often to be found grinning at gutters.

He constantly breaks school rule number 742: boys must not break school rules.

Ben thinks he can get away with anything by flashing his blue eyes and looking innocent. I am not fooled. Indeed I am still waiting for him and Max Black to write a note of apology to Mr Bucket the caretaker. Gluing his wellington boots to the staffroom ceiling was outrageous!

Head teacher - Hagatha Hogsbottom (Mrs)

Contents

1. Rain, Rain, Go Away!

Max Black and Ben Neal zoomed towards Oldacre Primary School in their imaginary spymobile.

"We're early today thanks to these supersonic booster engines," said Max as they skidded to a halt outside the church next door to the playground. "Plenty of time for our first mission: find our gargoyle friends."

Ben grinned. "Good thinking, Agent Black. We'll snoop around the churchyard before we go into school."

The old church was covered in

elaborate gargoylz – ancient stone statues that spouted rainwater from the gutters. Max and Ben were the only humans who knew that the funny little creatures were alive and that each had a special power. The gargoylz were now great friends with the boys and loved to play naughty tricks as much as they did.

The boys were about to race into the churchyard when Max suddenly spotted a familiar figure sitting on the playground bench. His spy radar leaped into action: pigtails bobbing, monitor's badge gleaming, smug smile all over her face. He

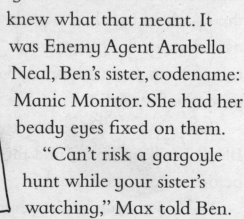

knew what that meant. It was Enemy Agent Arabella Neal, Ben's sister, codename: Manic Monitor. She had her beady eyes fixed on them.

"Can't risk a gargoyle hunt while your sister's watching," Max told Ben.

"We can soon scare her off," Ben whispered back. "We'll sneak up and put spiders—"

But before he could finish, the sky clouded over and it began to pour with rain. Arabella let out a shriek and fled for her classroom, clutching her PE bag over her head.

"Cool!" exclaimed Ben. "We didn't have to do anything!" He looked up, but the rain had stopped as abruptly as it had started.

"Girls are so silly," said Max pityingly. "What's wrong with a bit of water? Anyway, now the coast's clear we can search for the gargoylz."

"They're probably on the church, enjoying the downpour," said Ben.

The boys dashed along the churchyard path, scanning the ancient gutters.

"Not even a stone whisker!" said Max, disappointed.

 As he spoke, the rain came down again. His dark spiky hair was soon plastered to his head and Ben's trainers began to squelch.

"This weather's crazy," said Max as the boys dived into the church porch out of the rain.

A long stripy tail suddenly flopped down in front of them.

"Horrible weather," came a miserable voice from above.

The boys looked up at the beams and Max activated his radar: bristling whiskers, pointy cat's ears, small fangs. He knew what that meant. It was Theo, their gargoyle friend. Theo's special power was turning into a fierce tiger, but as he was just four hundred and twelve years old – young for a gargoyle – he hadn't got it quite right yet. So far, the best he could manage was a small fluffy kitten.

"What's the matter, Theo?" asked Max.
"There's plenty of rainwater to spout. We
thought you'd be out enjoying yourself."

"The others are," said Theo, scowling.
"They're on top of the tower having
spitting contests."

"We didn't look there,"
admitted Ben.

"Why didn't you go
with them, Theo?"
asked Max.

"Fierce tigers
don't like rain,"
explained Theo. "It stops
us doing our favourite
things, like chasing pigeons
off the weathervane."

"Theo's got a point," said
Ben thoughtfully. "Rain may
be good for getting rid of
annoying sisters, but I can't
skateboard when it's wet."

"And we're always called in from football when it rains," added Max, "even though puddles are fun."

They heard the sound of the school bell.

"Time to go," sighed Ben. "But don't worry, Theo. We'll think of a way to cheer you up. There's nothing like a cheering-up mission to stop us getting bored in class."

"We haven't had a single good idea all morning," moaned Ben as the boys left the dining room after lunch.

"The rain must have made our brains go soft," said Max.

"And Miss Bleet kept forcing us to get
on with our work," Ben went on. "She
wouldn't listen when I said I was too busy
to think about silly things like the nine
times table."

"There's only one thing for a soft brain,
Agent Neal," said Max as they ran into the
playground. "Football!"

"We're sure to think of something after
that!" agreed Ben.

But each time they got ready for the
kick-off, there was a sudden downpour

and everyone was called in.

"Fingers crossed!" exclaimed Max as the rain stopped and they started their third football game. "Let's hope we get to finish the Master Spies play Double Agents World Cup Final this time ... Uh-oh. Spoke too soon." The rain had started up again and the dinner ladies were shooing everyone in for the fourth time.

"Pretend we haven't heard," said Max through gritted teeth.

He was running up to score the winning

goal when there was a bellow from behind.
He checked his spy radar: grey hair, beaky
nose, face like an angry tomato. He knew
what that meant. It was Enemy Agent Mrs
Hogsbottom, commonly known as Mrs
Hogsbum, codename: Evil Head Teacher.
She was heading straight for them,
umbrella quivering.

"Max Black and Ben Neal!" she yelled.

"Get back inside immediately! You have broken school rule number two hundred and eighty-nine: boys must not make the head teacher leave her pasta salad and chase them in out of the rain."

"Theo was right about the rain," said Ben when they got back to their classroom. "It spoils everything. We'll never think of a way to cheer him up at this rate."

"I know why it's raining," said Max mysteriously.

"We all know that," said Ben. "Mr Widget went on about it in science class. It's when the clouds—"

"I mean, I know why it's raining *today*,"

Max interrupted. "When Mrs Hogsbum was chasing us in, I saw Ira on the church wall. He was flapping a wing, and you know what that means—"

"It's Ira who's making it rain!" exclaimed Ben. "Of course. It's his special gargoyle power. He's playing a trick!"

Max looked out of the window. "Rain's stopped again," he said. "That's because Ira can only do short bursts. Let's get out there quickly while there's still some playtime left and make him stop his silly pranks. *He* might think it's fun but nobody else does."

But when the boys reached Ira, they were surprised to see him looking as gloomy as Theo.

"Ahoy there, crew!" squawked the feathery gargoyle, fixing them with his piercing eyes. Ira looked a bit like a stone eagle – but he didn't sound like one. Ever since a seafaring parrot had landed on him years ago he'd decided to be a pirate.

"Ahoy there, Ira," replied Ben. "Good joke with the rain, but could you—"

"*Bad* joke, shipmates," said Ira, shaking his head sadly. "Worked well at Sports Day. Everyone abandoned ship – lots of bloodcurdling screams. Now no one's yelling at all, however wet they get. I'm a failure. I should be fed to the sharks!" He hid his hooked beak under his wing.

"You're not a failure," said Ben kindly.

"Your rainstorms are great! But a trick has to take people by surprise. Everyone's used to the rain now. Why don't you stop – then Max and I can play football?"

"Stop?" squawked Ira doubtfully. "Don't know about that. I've got nothing else to do."

"Tell you what," said Max. "If you stop making it rain, everyone will forget about it and we'll think of a really good trick for you to do when they're all nice and dry."

"All right then," agreed Ira, perking up. "But here's a pirate's warning – if it's a bad prank you'll walk the plank!"

He hopped away along the wall and the boys raced off to finish their game of football.

★ ★ ★

"Master Spies win the cup again, Agent Neal," said Max as he and Ben sauntered into the classroom covered in mud. "That was an awesome game. I'm glad Ira took our advice."

"Now we've got to think of a trick for him to play," answered Ben, "*and* cheer Theo up too."

"Max Black and Ben Neal," came a voice. "What *do* you think you look like?"

Max's spy radar whirred into action: short and dumpy, limp brown hair, head wobbling like a frightened chicken. It was Enemy Agent Miss Bleet, codename: Wimpy Teacher.

"Have you forgotten we're having the school photo this afternoon?" Miss Bleet asked in a panic. "You'd better clean your faces and smarten up!" The boys shuddered as she waved a brush at them.

"We can't touch that!" exclaimed Max, eyes wide. "Some girl might have used it."

"We'd smell all flowery," insisted Ben, backing away towards the wall. "And I've washed once this week already."

"My hair will go flat," added Max, feeling his spiky dark tangles.

There was a thud of footsteps in the corridor and the door was flung open. Before he could activate his radar, Mrs Hogsbottom burst in.

"General announcement!" she boomed.

"It's stopped raining so we'll have the school photo outside." She turned on her heel and was about to burst back out again when she spotted the two mud-splashed boys. Her eyes grew wide with shock.

"Outrageous!" she hissed. "Put them at the back of the photo."

As soon as she'd gone, Max turned to Ben. "I've had an idea," he whispered.

He dashed over to the window and peered up at the staffroom roof. Then he ran back and snatched the brush from Miss Bleet. He gave his hair a quick going over and tucked in his shirt – without being asked.

"Can I go to the toilet please?" he asked politely. "I'll wash my face there." He could see the look of

horror and confusion on Ben's face,
but explanations would have to wait.

Miss Bleet nodded and Max raced
upstairs. He stood on the seat of one of the
girls' toilets and stuck his head out of the
window. After all, Miss Bleet hadn't said
which toilet he could go to.

A monkey-like gargoyle with leafy
wings was crouched on the flat roof of the
staffroom below, giggling at the dinner
ladies as they straightened their whistles
ready for the photo.

"Toby!" whispered Max excitedly.
"Over here."

Toby grinned and flew up to the
window ledge beside him. Flying was

-18-

Toby's special power. "Greetingz!" he said in his growly purr. "What's up?"

"Can you pass a message on to Ira?" said Max. "I promised him he could do a trick, and this is going to be the best rainy trick in the history of rainy tricks!"

Toby's face fell. "I'm fed up with Ira's rain," he said gloomily. "It was fun at first but I don't want any more today. The church gutterz are overflowing."

"You'll love this trick," insisted Max. "We're having a school photo in a minute. Everyone's all neat and tidy – it's horrible. Anyway, I need Ira to be hiding nearby. When we're all ready, I'll wave my hand and—"

"Ira can make it rain and everyone will get soaked!" Toby's golden eyes flashed and he waved his dragony tail in delight. "Dangling drainpipes, that'll be great!"

"Tell him the harder the rain falls the better," said Max.

"I'll tell him now," said Toby. He took off, did a loop the loop and shot away towards the church.

"It's weird being clean in the middle of the day," grumbled Ben as the two boys trailed along behind their classmates towards the chairs set out for the photo. "We're going to look really stupid. Can't see why you're grinning about it."

"You needn't worry, Agent Neal," whispered Max. "No one will see us looking all clean and horrible because we won't be having our photos taken." He winked at Ben. "Ira's going to play a trick."

Ben looked at him blankly for a moment.

"With his . . . special power," said Max.

Ben's face broke into a broad grin as he worked it out. "That'll be cool!"

"And wet," added Max.

Year Four were ushered into their places with the rest of the school. Mrs Hogsbottom perched on her special head teacher's chair in the front, her beaky nose polished and every grey hair slapped into place. The teachers sat beside her. The infants sat cross-legged at the teachers' feet.

The sky was blue and the sun was shining.

Agent Max Black glanced up at the church. He could see Toby, Theo and Ira peeping over the wall, watching the action. He checked up and down the rows. The whole school was there, even Mrs Simmer and the kitchen staff. It was time to put the plan into action. He flapped his hand as if he was swatting a fly.

"Keep your hand still, that boy," said the photographer. Max put his hand down obediently. "Everyone say, *Smelly sausages.*"

"Smelly sausages!" chanted the school. As the photographer moved his finger towards the button, a small black cloud suddenly appeared right overhead. The rain poured down. Lightning flashed and thunder rolled. In an instant everyone was soaked.

Max and Ben high-fived.

"Outrageous!" bellowed Mrs Hogsbottom. She charged for the nearest door, herding pupils ahead of her like a bossy sheepdog.

Lucinda Tellingly and Tiffany Goodchild shrieked past, leading the class stampede.

"No running!" squeaked Miss Bleet, splashing through the puddles at the back.

"Success, Agent Black," said Ben as they
followed her inside.

"More like soak-cess, Agent Neal!"
replied Max, ruffling his hair to make
it stand up in spikes again. "Ira was
awesome!"

The minute school was finished the boys
raced out into the playground.

"Yo-ho-ho!" came a chirpy squawk
from the church wall. "Set sail for the seven
seas!" Ira's piercing eyes were peeping at
them.

"What did you think of the rain trick,
Ira?" called Max. "We won't have to walk
the plank now, will we?"

"Shiver me timbers!" said Ira. "Certainly
not. You did well . . . for a pair of
landlubbers."

Toby and Theo clambered onto the wall.

"Spluttering gutterz!" exclaimed Toby. "I haven't laughed so much since we cut holez in the vicar's umbrella. Good work, Ira."

But Ira's beak drooped. "Now everyone's gone home I've got no one to rain on." He waddled off miserably.

"We can't let him get gloomy again," said Theo, frowning. "We'll be flooded."

"I've had an idea about that," said Ben. "I've made up a game. It's called Stalking Ira." Theo looked puzzled. "You see, you're a sort of cat – I mean tiger," Ben went on, "and Ira is a bird. And everybody knows that tigers stalk birds . . ."

A huge smile spread over Theo's stripy face. "I can stalk!" he said brightly. "Watch."

Max grinned. "Go, Theo!"

Ira was slumped on
a gravestone. Theo
crept up on him . . .
and pounced!

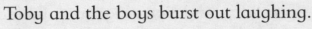

"Enemy astern!"
squawked Ira,
jumping into the air,
flapping his wings and
landing on his bottom.

Toby and the boys burst out laughing.

"I bet he wishes his special power was
flying now," chuckled Toby.

Ira gave them a grumpy look. "Avast
there," he screeched. "What do you scurvy
dogz find so funny?"

"Ben's invented a new game for Theo,"
called Max. "Why don't you join in?"

"Theo tries to catch you," Ben
explained. "And you have to escape before
he does."

Ira opened his beak and let out a happy
chirp. "Just let him try," he said. "This

shipmate's too fast for him."

"Oh, no you're not," yelled Theo, bounding at him across the churchyard.

Ira scrambled up one of the drainpipes and onto the roof, with Theo close behind. Theo pounced and Ira dodged out of his way. Theo slid across the wet tiles and got his head caught in a downspout. He pulled himself free and set off after Ira again.

Toby, Max and Ben laughed at their antics.

"Let's hope Theo keeps Ira busy for a long time," said Ben.

"Agreed," said Max. "Rain showers can be very useful, but we've had enough of that trick for today."

2. Science Project Panic

It was the last lesson on Tuesday, and Max and Ben were supposed to be doing science. But they were too excited. Year Four were going on a school outing on Friday and the boys couldn't think about anything else. In fact they'd been so busy talking about it, they'd only played one trick all day.

"I can't believe we're off to the beach!" exclaimed Max. "It's going to be the best school trip in the history of best school trips."

"A whole day of fossil hunting," said

Ben. "I'm going to find a T-Rex tooth."

"I'm going to dig up a whole T-Rex!" laughed Max.

"Max and Ben!"

Max's spy radar whirred into action. Small, twitchy, with sharp eyes that didn't miss a thing. Max knew what that meant. It was Enemy Agent Mrs

SPY FILE:

Code name:
Strict
Supply
Teacher

Stearn, codename: Strict Supply Teacher, who came in to take them every time Miss Bleet was away.

Miss Bleet had gone home sick at lunch time and was having the rest of the week off. For some reason she'd taken her chair with her. Max and Ben were sure it had nothing to do with them covering the seat with glue just before she sat on it!

The boys hated it when Mrs Stearn

took the class. She made them work really hard.

The supply teacher loomed over them. "I hope you're discussing the project you've been doing this term on earthquakes and volcanoes. What presentation are you going to make to the class tomorrow?"

"Presentation?" said Ben, aghast. "We were talking about the school trip."

"At this rate you two won't be going!" Mrs Stearn snapped.

"What do you mean?" gasped Max.

"You have to work hard to earn a treat like that," said Mrs Stearn, "and you clearly haven't been listening to me at all this afternoon. The whole class is to work in pairs and prepare a Show and Tell for tomorrow. You and Ben Neal will explain exactly how a volcano works."

She frowned at them. "I'm giving you fair warning. You'd better come up with an extra-special project or you'll both be staying here with me on Friday."

Ben flashed his blue eyes at Mrs Stearn and put on his innocent look. It always worked on the dinner ladies, who gave him extra pizza. It never worked on Mrs Stearn. The strict supply teacher simply raised an eyebrow and walked away.

The bell for the end of school rang loudly but Max and Ben hardly heard it. They were gawping at each other in disbelief.

"This is serious, Agent Neal," muttered Max. "Our whole happiness depends on this presentation."

"We've only got one evening," Ben muttered back. "And we don't know anything about volcanoes."

They mooched out gloomily after the rest of the class and trailed across the playground.

"Psssst!"

Max looked over at the churchyard wall. Two pairs of eyes and four pointy ears were peeping over the top. "It's Toby and Barney," he said. "Maybe they can cheer us up."

They walked slowly over towards their gargoyle friends.

"Greetingz!" Toby beamed and swished his dragony tail. "Why are you looking so miserable?"

Barney's soppy dog face looked anxious and the spikes on his back quivered. "Has something terrible happened?" he asked.

"Not yet!" said Max. "But Friday looks doomed. Anyway, you're not to worry, Barney. We don't want you doing one of your pongs!"

Barney's secret gargoyle power was making revolting smells. When he was worried, he sometimes did them by accident.

The boys told Toby and Barney about the project and how they might miss their day out.

"I've got an idea!" Toby grinned. "Barney and I will help you. Four heads are better than two."

"And two tails," added Barney. "And eight paws."

"Great idea!" Max pulled open his backpack. "Hop in," he said. "We'll go to my house. It's nearer than Ben's."

Toby jumped in, then Barney climbed into Ben's bag and the boys set off for Max's house.

"Can Ben stay for tea, Mum?" asked Max as soon as they got through the front door. "We've got a project to do."

"Of course he can," said Max's mum. "I'll let your mother know, Ben."

"Tea!" came Toby's muffled voice from Ben's backpack. "Spluttering gutterz! I hope there are cookiez."

Max's mum stared in astonishment at Ben, who quickly licked his lips and rubbed his tummy.

"Of course there are," she said. "As long as you don't eat too many."

"Ten for me!" came the voice.

"Only joking!" said Ben hurriedly.

The boys grabbed some cookies and escaped upstairs. The moment Max's bedroom door was shut, Toby and Barney scrambled out, snatched a cookie each and started bouncing on the bed.

"You're here to help us with our project," Max reminded them. "So no messing about. Let's see if I've got any books about volcanoes . . ."

Barney scampered up Max's shelves and pulled down a book. "Never mind volcanoes," he said, holding up a picture of a huge dragon. "Tell the class that gargoylz have got better tailz than these silly-looking creaturez."

"But that's not what the project's about," protested Ben.

"Read them this joke . . ." chortled Toby, peering at a comic he'd found under Max's bed. "*What's brown and sticky?*"

"I don't know," said Barney. "What *is* brown and sticky?"

"*A stick!*" shrieked Toby.

The two gargoylz rolled around on their backs, helpless with laughter.

"Must tell Bart," spluttered Barney. "He loves a good joke."

"And *that* was a good joke!" agreed Toby.

"You're meant to be looking up volcanoes," sighed Max.

Toby and Barney found a book on worms, turned it upside down and stuck their noses in it.

"Wow!" whispered Ben in admiration.

"They're even worse than we are at homework – and that's saying something!"

Max pulled a book called *Deadly Mountains* down from his shelf and opened it. "I can't understand these long words," he complained, staring at a complicated diagram of the inside of a volcano. "I thought it would just be *boom* and *bang*!"

"My head hurts," groaned Ben. "Homework isn't good for you."

"Teachers are cruel to even think of it. We need a rest." Max switched on his television and flicked through the channels. "Hey, this is lucky. Here's a programme all about volcanoes! Awesome."

The boys threw themselves onto the bed and the gargoylz squeezed in between. Together they watched the mountain on the screen erupt in an explosion of lava.

"Dangling drainpipes!" said Toby when the programme ended. "That was fun."

"Volcanoes are amazing!" gasped Max. "We must be able to impress the class tomorrow."

"But Mrs Stearn wants us to tell them all the boring details," sighed Ben. "If only we could just show them that programme."

Max jumped to his feet. "I've got it, Agent Neal," he cried. "We won't talk.

We'll make a model and *demonstrate* how a volcano erupts!"

"Brilliant plan, Agent Black," said Ben. "That should be easy-peasy. We've seen how they spout lava."

"We'll help," said Toby, waddling to the edge of the bed. "Gargoylz are experts on spouting – well, with water anyway."

"We just need the things to make the model." Max looked around his room, thinking furiously. "I know what to use for the volcano shape – my sister's witch hat. Urgent mission, Agent Neal: go into the dangerous territory of Jessica's bedroom and grab the hat."

"It will smell clean and flowery and horrible," said Ben, looking grave. "But I'll do it!"

"Hold your nose and you'll be all right," said Max. "I'm going to the kitchen. I've got a mission of my own – fetching the perfect ingredient for our volcano lava. Gargoylz, stay here."

Max crept down the stairs and into the kitchen. He grabbed the tomato ketchup bottle, stuffed it up his jumper and then dashed back upstairs to his room.

A small figure stood
in the middle of the
bedroom, wrapped
in toilet paper.
Toby's eyes peered
out. "I got this from
the bathroom,"
he explained in a
muffled voice. "But
I had trouble getting
it off the wall. I thought
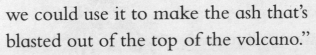
we could use it to make the ash that's
blasted out of the top of the volcano."

"Good thinking!" said Max. "But I told
you to stay here, Toby. What if someone
had seen you running about looking like
an Egyptian mummy?"

Ben burst in, wearing the witch's hat.
"I found it at the bottom of Jessica's
wardrobe," he complained as he plonked it
down on the floor, "behind her fluffy pink
slippers."

"Yuck!" said Max. He looked around in a sudden panic. "Where's Barney?"

A pile of clothes in the corner of the room wriggled, and Barney's head popped out. He waved a green jumper at the boys. "Let's put this around the bottom of the volcano," he said. "It'll look like a forest."

"Brilliant idea." Max grinned. "I've never liked that jumper and Mum can't complain if I'm using it for science." He pulled a large framed picture of a waterfall from under his bed. "My great-aunt sent me this at Christmas," he explained. "It's as bad as the jumper. We can use it as the base." He rummaged on his shelf and threw Barney a tube of glue.

They set to work. When the hat was stuck firmly to the base, Max got out a pot and a brush and slapped brown paint over the hat's shiny surface. The paint didn't stick very well so it was a bit patchy, but Toby stuck blobs of toilet paper onto it to look like ash. Meanwhile Barney pulled some woollen threads out of the green jumper and arranged them around the bottom of the volcano, then Ben splattered ketchup over the top.

"Mmm . . . this lava tastes good," murmured Toby, sticking a paw in and licking it.

At last the model was finished.

Max, Ben and the gargoylz sat down on the messy carpet to survey their work. The volcano looked quite good until, under the weight of wet paint, ketchup and toilet paper, the hat slowly sank into a soggy heap.

"It's not *quite* like the volcano on the telly," sighed Max. "What's Mrs Stearn going to say?"

"Perhaps it needs more paint—" Ben began, then stopped in horror because they could all hear footsteps on the stairs.

"Tea's ready," came Mum's voice.

"She mustn't see the state of my room!" hissed Max, trying to wipe ketchup smears off his wardrobe. "I'll be grounded for life."

"I've got an idea," said Ben. "Quick, Barney, make one of your pongs!"

Barney chuckled, and a stench like rotting socks rose up into the air – just as Max's mum opened the door.

"**Euuwww!** Did you have to, boys?" she gasped, staggering back out of the room. "Come down for tea – and no more smells."

They heard her coughing all the way downstairs.

"That was awesome, Barney," said Max, throwing

open the window. "You saved us from a fate worse than death!"

"It was your worst— I mean, best pong yet," spluttered Ben, wafting the smell out with a pillow.

"We'd better go down for tea." Max turned to Toby and Barney. "You two try to be good while we're gone."

"Of course," said Toby. "We'll tidy up for you."

Twenty minutes later Max flung open the door of his bedroom and stared in horror.

The carpet had disappeared under a pile of shredded toilet paper, there were tomato ketchup paw prints all over his duvet, and someone had painted a splodgy picture of a brown gargoyle on his rucksack. Barney and Toby sat in the middle of the chaos, happily watching cartoons.

"We told you we'd tidy up." Toby pointed proudly towards the bin, where the remains of the green jumper had been stuffed.

"It looks worse than ever!" wailed Max.

DER-RING! The front doorbell sounded. They heard running footsteps on the stairs and the bedroom door swung open. Ben just had time to throw the duvet over the gargoylz before Max's dad came in.

"Ben, your mum's—" Max's dad stopped. He gawped speechlessly at Max's room.

Then he spotted the collapsed volcano. "What have you done to Jessica's hat?" he demanded angrily.

"We've got a science project," Max tried to explain, "and we thought it would be great to make a model for the whole class to see, but it didn't quite work.

It's meant to be a volcano . . ." He tailed off miserably. It had all gone wrong. Their hopes of going on the school trip had gone down the drain and now they were in big trouble.

Dad looked serious. "I see," he said, solemnly examining the soggy mess. "It's a bit flat for a volcano – and it looks as if someone's eaten most of the lava." He scratched his head. "Look, I'm really pleased to see you've been working so hard for a school project so I'll help you out. I've got a sheet of thin metal in the garage. I can make that into a cone shape for you. It'll be much stronger than a cardboard hat. You can slap

papier-mâché on it and then paint it to
look like a real volcano – but only if you
clean up this mess first. Deal?"

"Deal!" cried the boys happily.

"And I'll make Ben's mum a cuppa
while she waits," added Dad as he went
out.

"That was a lucky escape," said Max.
"If it had been Mum she'd be telling us
off for about a million years. Good thing
Dad's mad about science."

"Let's get cleaning," said Ben.

Toby and Barney popped up from
under the duvet.

"We'll help," said Toby. "We'll do the
best job since we put soap powder
in the font and the vicar got
covered in bubblez!"

"Thanks, gargoylz." Max
grinned. "But first *you* need
a wipe. You're both covered
in ketchup."

3. Fire! Fire!

Max and Ben shuffled slowly along to
school in their imaginary spy hovercraft,
carefully carrying their science project
between them. They had to get the
precious model to the classroom in one
piece or they'd miss the school trip to the
beach on Friday.

"Looks awesome, doesn't it, Agent
Neal?" Max grinned over the red-painted
peak of their volcano.

"You bet, Agent Black," said Ben.

With the help of Max's dad they'd made
a magnificent fiery-topped mountain with

papier-mâché sides and realistic-looking lava oozing down its slopes.

The boys sidled through the school gates.

"We're early," said Ben. "Let's show this to the gargoylz. They'll be really impressed."

They wobbled over to the wall between the school and the churchyard and balanced their volcano carefully on the top.

"I can't see anyone," said Max, disappointed.

"I can hear something," said Ben. "They must be behind that gravestone."

"What do you call a greedy ant?" came a deep gurgly voice.

"That's Bart," whispered Max. "He's telling jokes as usual."

"An anteater!" Gales of gargoyle giggles echoed around the churchyard.

"Gargoylz . . ." Ben called softly.

Five beaming faces peeped over the tombstone.

"Greetingz," said Toby, flying over to them. Barney, Theo and Azzan scampered after him, and Bart waddled along behind, straightening his gladiator skirt.

"What do you call that mountain thingy?" asked Theo, jumping up

onto the wall like a cat and peering at the volcano.

"I don't know, Theo," said Bart. "What *do* you call that mountain thingy? I haven't heard that joke before."

"It's not a joke this time," giggled Theo, pointing at the model. "I want to know what the boyz have got there."

Bart stared at it, puzzled. "It looks like one of the vicar's dinnerz."

"It's not for eating," said Ben. "It's a volcano."

"What's a volcano?" grunted Bart.

"We know, don't we, Toby?" said Barney with a shy grin.

"It's a mountain that breathes fire!" explained Toby.

"*I* breathe fire," said Azzan, gleaming with pride. "Make your volcano do it now."

"Only real ones do that," said Ben. "Ours is just a model."

Max grabbed his arm. "But wouldn't it be awesome if it *did* breathe fire, Agent Neal?" he said. "Imagine Mrs Stearn's face! It would be the best project in the history of best projects. She'd have to let us go on the school trip then!"

"Awesome idea," said Ben thoughtfully.

"But how would we get the volcano to do that?"

Max grinned and pointed at Azzan. "We could ask for help. Breathing fire is Azzan's special power."

"I like your thinking!" exclaimed Ben. He turned to the little dragon gargoyle. "Do you want to be part of a really wicked trick, Azzan?"

"Gargoylz love to play tricks," Azzan replied, jumping up and down.

"Then it's time for Secret Plan: Blast Fire!" Max told the eager gargoyle. "You hide underneath the volcano, and when I call out a secret codeword, you blast fire out through the top."

"Spluttering gutterz!" exclaimed Toby. "That's a brilliant idea!"

But then Azzan stopped jumping.
"There's one tiny problem," he
said, twisting his paws together in
embarrassment. "I don't always manage
fire. Sometimez it's only a wisp of smoke.
And when I do breathe fire, it doesn't last
very long."

"Don't you worry about that," Ben told
him. "It will still be awesome. No one will
be expecting smoke or flames at all."

"Then I'll do it!" declared Azzan
excitedly.

Bart was shaking his head doubtfully.
"It won't work," he said. "Azzan's too big
to fit inside."

"If you put the volcano on top of a box,
Azzan could hide underneath," suggested

Toby. "You'd
just need to
cut a hole in
the top of the box
under the volcano."

"That's brilliant,
Toby!" said Max.

Azzan skipped along the wall.

But Ben looked worried. "If he breathes
fire inside a cardboard box, he'll set fire to
it," he said.

"I hadn't thought of that," said Max,
scratching his head. "Perhaps our plan
won't work after all."

"Leave this to me," said Azzan
importantly. Waving the others aside, he
inspected the model volcano closely. He
tapped it thoughtfully with one claw. Then
he hopped over it and tapped the other
side. Finally he lifted it up and stuck his
nose underneath.

Max, Ben and the gargoylz watched

anxiously. At last Azzan's head popped up again. "Just as I thought." He grinned. "Once I'm in the box I can stick my head through the hole in the top and up into the volcano itself. That's made of metal so it won't catch fire."

"This is going to be cool!" exclaimed Ben. "Secret Plan: Blast Fire! is on!"

The bell rang for school.

"We have to go," said Max. "We'll see you here at lunch time to finalize the plan. We have to present our project this afternoon."

"We'll find a cardboard box," declared Theo.

"Great," said Ben. "All sorted."

The boys picked up their model and shuffled off into school.

At lunch time Max and Ben carried their
volcano over to the church wall again,
where the gargoylz were waiting eagerly.
Barney proudly produced a cardboard box
bearing the label – CRUMBLY COOKIES.

"I found this in the school kitchens," he
said. "I made sure it was empty for you."
He licked his lips. "They were delicious!"

"We just need
a hole for Azzan
to stick his head
through now," said Ben.
He patted the cardboard. "It's tough.
How are we going to cut it? We can't risk
bringing scissors outside. If we got caught

there'd be no school trip no matter how
good our volcano was."

"Stand back, everyone!" ordered Azzan.
He took a deep breath. **Whoosh!** A huge
flame shot out and hit the top of the box.
The cardboard began to crackle. Azzan
quickly flapped at it with his tail. "Perfect!"
he declared as the flames died away,
leaving a smoking hole.

CRUMBLY
COOKIES

The gargoylz clapped.
Azzan bowed and
jumped into the box.
"Ow!" He
jumped out again,
clutching his bottom.
"Think I'll wait till
it's cooled down a bit."
When the box was
ready, Azzan got in again.
He curled his long tail around him, and
Max placed the volcano carefully on top.

"Does it fit all right?" called Ben.

"It's perfect," came Azzan's muffled
voice. "Ready for action."

"Listen for the password," Max told him,
peering down the top of the volcano. "You
breathe fire when I say *Blast off*." A small
flame flickered out of the volcano, making
him jump backwards. "Brilliant! But not
now!" he exclaimed. "Wait till I say it in
the classroom."

★ ★ ★

That afternoon Max and Ben could
hardly sit still. Their volcano stood on their
desk, covered with a coat.

Lucinda Tellingly and Tiffany
Goodchild were reading out an endless
description of earthquakes.

"Boring!" muttered Ben. "When's it our
turn?"

Lucinda glared at them.

"Did you say something, Ben Neal?" asked Mrs Stearn.

"I'm just looking forward to showing everyone how volcanoes work," said Ben.

"Then you can be next," the teacher told them. "After all, your school trip depends on it."

As soon as the girls had finished, Max and Ben jumped up eagerly. They carried the volcano up to the front and put it on the teacher's table. Then Max removed the coat with a flourish.

Mrs Stearn looked astonished. "I wasn't expecting anything like this from you two," she gasped. "You *have* worked hard!"

"And there are more surprises to come," said Ben with a grin.

Max turned to the class. "The volcano!" he announced dramatically. "Nature at its fiercest." He'd heard that on the TV programme.

"Here it waits, looking like a harmless mountain," said Ben, "but prepare yourselves for an amazing sight."

Max took a step back. "Hold onto your seats and get ready for . . . *Blast off!*"

He waited, but nothing happened.

"Blast off?" said Mrs Stearn, puzzled. "You're getting muddled up with rockets, boys."

"Yes, of course," said Max. "I didn't mean to say *Blast off* at all."

A small wisp of smoke rose up from the model. To the boys' delight, the supply teacher looked impressed.

"How did you do that?" she asked.

"Well, it's very complicated and clever . . ." began Max, wondering how he was going to explain without telling her there was a fire-breathing gargoyle inside.

"I don't see why it's so clever," piped up Lucinda. "It was only a little bit of smoke. Ben promised it was going to be amazing!"

"That was just the beginning," said Ben, looking desperately at Max. "Er . . . volcanoes do that . . . They smoke first before the big eruption."

"Was it talcum powder?" asked Mrs Stearn. "Or flour?" She was peering eagerly into the hole now. "I'm determined to discover how you did it . . ."

Max was horrified. He had to stop her spotting Azzan!

"Sorry, but it's top secret," he said hurriedly. "You'd better stand back, miss. It could *blast off* at any moment."

Before Mrs Stearn had a chance to move, a puff of black smoke shot up her nose. She lurched backwards as a huge flame leaped into the air.

Lucinda and Tiffany screamed but the rest of the class clapped enthusiastically. Max and Ben took several bows.

"Awesome, Azzan!" shouted Ben as the flames flickered merrily out of the volcano.

Max kicked him on the shin.

"I mean, it's as awesome *as an* . . . actual volcano," Ben corrected himself hurriedly.

But Mrs Stearn wasn't listening.

Eyes wide with terror at the sight of the crackling flames, she grabbed a vase of flowers from her desk and threw the water over the volcano.

Pffftttt. The flames went out. Max and Ben stared at each other in horror. Their model was covered in wet carnation stalks and smelly leaves. The painted

papier-mâché was peeling
away and dripping
onto the floor. Their
volcano project was
ruined.

"It's really
realistic now,"
Lucinda giggled
nastily. "All that
stuff running down
looks like real lava."

From the depths of the soggy model
came sounds of spluttering and wheezing.

Max burst into a volley of deafening
coughs to cover up the sound. "The smoke
got in my throat," he explained quickly.

He and Ben picked up the ruined
volcano to take it back to their seat.

"Wait a minute," said Mrs Stearn,
looking rather embarrassed. "I'm sorry I
spoiled your volcano. It was a very good
effort and the flames were . . . a clever idea.

Just a little dangerous perhaps . . . but I'm sure you meant well."

"We did," said Max despondently. "It took us hours to make it."

"Then you have earned your place on Friday's trip," said the supply teacher with a smile. "And as I ruined your project, I will let you off homework for a week!"

Lucinda and Tiffany looked appalled, but Max and Ben broke into beaming smiles.

"Mission accomplished, Agent Neal," whispered Max when they were sitting down. "The trip to the beach is safe."

"*And* no homework!" Ben whispered back in delight.

Max knocked on the box. "You all right in there, Azzan?"

A thin wisp of steam drifted up from the

top of the volcano. "Just a little damp," came the muffled reply.

After school the boys carried the volcanic remains into the churchyard. Azzan scrambled out of the wreckage as the other gargoylz gathered round.

"What happened?" asked Barney, round-eyed with dismay at the ruined model. "Did it go wrong?"

"Not at all," declared Azzan. "It was just like those volcanoes you told us about. But better!"

"Much better," agreed Max. "We couldn't have done it without him – and you lot, of course."

"I'm sorry you got wet, Azzan," added Ben. "Mrs Stearn didn't understand. Typical teacher!"

"Think no more about it," said Azzan, flicking his tail happily. "I could hear the class clapping. I haven't had so much fun since we turned on the fire extinguisher and the vicar thought it was snowing!"

Toby sighed. "Wish we could have seen it."

"You can," declared Max. "You keep the model here and Azzan can act it out for you tonight."

"Dangling drainpipes!" exclaimed Toby. "Hop back in, Azzan."

"I'll say the password," said Theo quickly.

Toby took charge. "You can say it this time," he told him, "then we'll all have a turn."

Laughing, Max and Ben left the gargoylz happily shouting "*Blast off!*" and headed for home.

4. Fossil Fun

"I can't believe it's time for the school trip at last!" yelled Max as he and Ben roared into the playground in their imaginary super spy plane.

"There's only one thing that could make a day on the beach even better," said Ben.

"Our gargoyle friends coming with us!" Max grinned. "Shame they can't. We'll just have to tell them all about it when we get back." He glanced over the wall at the church next door. "No sign of them," he declared, feeling a little disappointed. "I thought they'd come and see us off."

Just then, Mr Widget blew his whistle.
All the Year Four pupils lined up by
the gate and streamed onto the coach,
laughing and jostling. Max and Ben beat
Lucinda and her friends to the long seat at
the back.

"I saw Theo
and Barney on
the church roof when
we left," Max told Ben as the
coach sped along. "They looked a
bit gloomy."

"Maybe the gargoylz are upset 'cos
they can't come," said Ben.

"Can't come?" said a deep growly voice.

A stony face poked out from under the
seat in front. It had a wide mouth and the
sharpest fangs the boys had ever seen. The
strange gargoyle clambered up Max's legs
and perched on his knee. He was small
and stocky, with the body of a
piglet. "Who's going to
stop us?"

"Not me!" quavered Max as he and
Ben shrank back at the sight of this fierce
new gargoyle.

Pop! Zack suddenly appeared out of
thin air on the seat between them. Zack's
special power was becoming invisible and

the boys never
knew when he
might turn up.

"You boyz
look terrified!" he
guffawed, shaking
his fuzzy mane. "It's
only Cyrus. Say
hello, Cyrus."

The new
gargoyle held out
a paw full of razor-sharp claws. Max and
Ben shook it very carefully.

"Nice to meet you," said Ben politely.

"You'll have to stay out of sight," Max
warned the two gargoylz. "You know you
mustn't be seen by humans – except us,
that is."

"We will!" came a whole chorus of
voices.

Shocked, Max and Ben peered under
their seat. They were greeted by a row

of eyes blinking in the dark. Five more grinning gargoylz shuffled into view.

"Bart . . . Toby . . . Eli . . . Ira . . . Azzan," gasped Max, counting along the line.

"Brilliant!" exclaimed Ben. "You're nearly all here."

"Greetingz!" said Toby, dusting himself down. "We tried to persuade Theo to come but he doesn't like water. And Barney said he'd stay behind to keep him company."

"We've never been to the seaside," said Bart.

"Speak for yourself, landlubber!" chirped Ira.

The girls in the seat in front turned round and stared.

Max quickly gave them a cheesy grin. "Just doing my pirate impression!" he assured them.

"Shhhh!" Ben warned the stowaway gargoylz. "You don't want to be discovered."

"Max and Ben are the only humanz allowed to see us," Toby solemnly reminded his friends.

"You're lucky to have an old sea dog like me on a trip to the coast," Ira went on in a hoarse whisper. "You'd be lost if a force nine gale or a monster from the deep came along."

"Ssso would you!"
hissed Eli with a grin,
the stone snakes on
his head wriggling
cheekily.

"You black-
hearted serpent,"
growled Ira. "I've
got the sea in
my blood. You'll
soon be calling me
for help when you're
sucked into a whirlpool."

The gargoylz chattered excitedly all the
way to the beach. Every so often Max or
Ben had to remind them to be quiet.

"Everyone ready?" called Mr Widget
from the front after about half an hour.
"We're nearly there."

"Line up, you motley crew," squawked
Ira. The gargoylz shuffled into an orderly
queue behind him. "We've been watching

you all in the playground," Ira explained proudly to the boys.

"You do it very well," whispered Max, impressed. "Better than us!"

"But you can't march out with the rest of us," warned Ben. "You'll be seen. Stay put until everyone's off the coach. We'll see you on the beach."

Max and Ben were the last down the steps of the coach; they joined the rest of Year Four at the top of the cliff path.

"Awesome!" gasped Ben, gazing down at the wide, sunny bay that stretched out invitingly below them.

"Bet there are loads of fossils hidden down there," said Max, pointing at the rocks that lay in a heap against the foot of the cliff. "And we're going to find them all."

Mr Widget climbed back into the coach to check that no one had been left behind.

"Hope the gargoylz have got out!" muttered Ben.

They heard a sharp exclamation and the teacher emerged, his hair standing on end.

"Everything all right, sir?" asked Max. Mr Widget mopped his brow. "I thought I saw a face under the seat – huge mouth, fierce teeth. Terrifying!"

"Probably just a trick of the light," said Ben quickly, trying not to laugh as a line of honey-coloured shapes clambered out of the open coach window behind Mr Widget and gave the boys a cheery wave. Luckily the rest of Year Four were all gazing out at the sea.

Mr Widget shakily led the two classes down the steep concrete steps to the beach, where they saw a tall thin man with a bulging rucksack at his feet waving a chisel at them.

"Good morning, fossil hunters!" he called cheerily. "I'm Professor Bone." He began arranging interesting lumps of rock on the sand. "First of all, who can tell me what a fossil is?"

Ben put up his hand eagerly. "It's a—"

"Prehistoric creature that's turned to stone," a rude voice beside him butted in.

91

Max turned to look,
his spy radar on full alert:
shaved head, big fists,
nasty grin. He knew
what that meant. It was
Enemy Agent Barry
Price, also known as
The Basher, codename:
School Bully.

Codename:
School
Bully

"Exactly!" The professor beamed at
Barry, then held up a rock with a spiral
shape in the middle of it. "I found all these
here on this beach. Do you know what
this one is?" he asked Max.

"Easy," replied Max. "It's—"

"An ammonite," interrupted Barry with
an evil smirk in Max's direction.

"I see we have an expert here," chuckled
Professor Bone. "Ammonites used to swim
in these oceans sixty-five million years
ago." He tipped a pile of sharp, triangular
teeth into his hand. "These are from

92

prehistoric sharks," he told his wide-eyed audience. "There are plenty of fossils of all sorts around here. Some are loose in the sand and some will be in the rocks. Just keep your eyes open for unusual patterns in the stone and let's see who can find the best ones."

Excited chatter broke out at this.

"That'll be me," shouted Barry over the din. "You lot needn't bother."

He charged off and began to scour the sand. The rest of Year Four followed his lead and scattered across the beach. Soon sand was flying everywhere.

"Basher's such a spoilsport," complained Max as the boys clambered over the rocks they'd seen from the cliff path.

"We'll show him, Agent Black," said Ben, turning over some loose stones. "With our super spying skills we'll sniff out the biggest fossil in the history of biggest fossils. The Basher will be green with envy."

"Maybe the gargoylz will help, Agent Neal," added Max. "Wonder where they are."

"Behind you!" came a ferocious growl. Max and Ben spun round in alarm.

Cyrus and the rest of the gargoylz were watching them from behind a large rock, big grins on their faces.

"You're just in time," Max told them, trying to pretend he hadn't been scared at all. "We're on a fossil hunt."

"We'll help! We'll help!" shouted Zack, running up and down and sticking his nose in the sand. "Er . . . what's a fossil?"

"It's a type of pirate," said Ira knowledgeably.

"Not exactly," laughed Ben.

As soon as he had told the gargoylz what to look out for, they were off over the rocks. All except Ira, who hopped up onto a boulder. "I'll stay in the crow's nest," he squawked, shading his eyes with one wing, "and keep a weather eye out for enemy attack."

In no time a huge pile of seaweed and shells had mysteriously appeared on the sand next to the boys.

Pop! Zack came into view, his paws full of driftwood. "We're champion collectors!" he declared.

"Treasure!" squawked Ira in delight. "Pieces of eight!"

"Er . . . thanks, gargoylz," said Ben, looking doubtfully at the pile of wood as Zack vanished again. He winked at Max. "I don't think we're going to find the best fossil anywhere in this lot."

But Max was scraping at something in the sand. "Look what I've got!" he said, holding up a vicious-looking shark's tooth. "That must have been some fish! This fang's bigger than my hand! There's no way The Basher will do better than that."

"Everyone over here, please!" Mr
Widget called. He was standing on an
upturned bucket and waving
urgently at the diggers.
"Time to hand in
your best fossils."

"Let's show the tooth," said Ben. "The
professor will be knocked out."

But at that moment they heard heavy
footsteps on the sand behind them.

"Man the guns!" shrieked Ira. "We're
under attack!" He hopped behind a rock
just as The Basher pounded up to the pile
of driftwood.

"What a load of rubbish!" he snarled. Then he spotted Max's prize find. His eyes lit up. "I'm having that."

He snatched the shark's tooth right out of Max's hand and sprinted off towards Mr Widget, scattering groups of fossil finders as he went.

"What a cheat!" gasped Ben.

The gargoylz crept out from behind the rocks and Ira reappeared on his lookout perch. They all watched in dismay as Professor Bone praised Barry and displayed the tooth for Year Four to admire.

"That wasn't fair," complained Toby crossly.

"He's a scurvy sea dog!" exclaimed Ira.

"Right, he's not going to spoil our fun any more," said Max. "Let's build a super secret spy base over there, out of sight."

With the help of their gargoyle friends, the boys soon had a fantastic spy headquarters made out of sand. It had a castle tower, a rocket launcher and an underground communications centre covered in shells.

Ira tried to draw a skull and crossbones on the tower with his beak. Suddenly he stopped. "Enemy to starboard! Enemy to starboard!" he squawked, flapping his wings.

Everyone stopped digging.

"It's Barry again," hissed Max urgently, "and he's coming this way. Hide, gargoylz!"

Pop! Zack vanished and the others scuttled out of sight. Max and Ben stood on guard in front of the spy base.

"What a lovely castle!" said Barry, grinning spitefully. Suddenly he gave the boys a hard shove and they toppled backwards – right on top of their creation.

Barry guffawed
and whirled
away like
a tornado
towards his
next victim.

"He's such a
bully," muttered Max,
scrambling out of the
ruins of their spy base.

"Time someone taught him a
lesson," agreed Ben, shaking sand out of
his ear.

Toby scuttled over. "If I had my catapult
I'd get him," he said crossly.

"I could breathe fire and singe his
bottom!" declared Azzan.

"Someone might see you," Ben pointed
out.

"What about me?" said Cyrus, grinning
from ear to ear. "I could use my special
power."

"Is it something really scary?" asked
Ben hopefully.

"Not at all," said the fierce little
gargoyle. "I sing."

Max frowned. "I don't want to be rude,
but how will that help?"

"Cyrus's songs are
lullabies," explained
Toby.

"And when
he sssings one it
puts humanz to
sssleep. At once,"
added Eli.

"That's
brilliant!" Max grinned. "The Basher can't
be a bully if he's *asleep*!"

Barry was now busy throwing Lucinda's
shell collection into the sea. Cyrus
crept towards him and hid behind a tall
sandcastle where no one could see him.
Then he flung out his arms, opened his

mouth to show all his pointed teeth, and began to sing. Beautiful notes filled the air.

"It's so . . . sweet . . ." Max yawned as the melody washed over him.

"Wish I'd brought my pillow," murmured Ben dreamily.

"Cover your earsss!" hissed Eli urgently. "Or you'll fall asssleep as well."

Max and Ben quickly stuffed their fingers in their ears and watched as Barry gradually slumped to his knees, curled up on the sand and then began to snore. Cyrus finished his lullaby and scuttled back.

The boys took their fingers out of their ears.

"It's gone very quiet," said Ben.

"That's because the singing has worked on everyone!" exclaimed Max. "Look!"

Year Four, their teachers and Professor Bone were all stretched out on the beach, fast asleep.

"Awesome!" said Ben. "We've got the rest of the day to ourselves. What shall we do?"

"Wait a minute." Max turned to Cyrus. "How long will they all stay asleep?"

"Oh, ages!" declared Cyrus fiercely. "Probably all week."

"Ten minutes at most," Toby whispered to Max.

Max looked around at the sleeping figures. "We haven't got long before they wake up then."

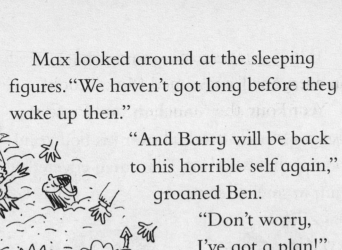

"And Barry will be back to his horrible self again," groaned Ben.

"Don't worry, I've got a plan!" said Max. "Let's bury him up to his neck in the sand. When he wakes up, he won't be able to move and we can have fun without him spoiling everything."

"Get digging, landlubbers!" ordered Ira. "All hands to the pump!"

Barry was now lying on his back, sucking his thumb.

As fast as they could, the boys and the gargoylz piled sand all over his body and patted it down hard. Then they covered him in smelly seaweed.

Ira perched on The Basher's chest and glared at him. "Next time it'll be the plank for you, my lad!" he squawked fiercely.

"Good work, everyone," said Ben, stepping back to admire the job. "It'll take Barry ages to get out of that."

"Keep an eye on the landlubbers!" warned Ira.

"They're getting out of their hammocks!"

"I think he means everyone's waking up," explained Ben.

As Year Four and the teachers got to their feet, still yawning, the boys could hear angry shouts from Barry, who was struggling in vain to stand up.

"Leave the dog there a while," advised Ira. "Teach him a lesson."

"Let's play hide-and-seek around the rock pools," said Max. "That'll keep the gargoylz hidden from view. I'll count first."

Ben and the gargoylz shot off to hide.

"Ready or not, here I come," called Max when he got to a hundred.

He leaped over a breakwater and landed on top of Ben. "One down, seven to go!" he declared as Ben joined in the search.

Pop! Zack suddenly appeared in front of them.

"You're supposed to be hiding," exclaimed Max, skidding to a halt.

"Clawz and pincers!" wailed Zack, in a panic. "Clawz and pincers!" The other gargoylz peeped out of their hiding places to see what was going on. Zack suddenly shot off around a rock pool and then vanished again. His stone friends burst out laughing.

"What's going on?" asked Max, puzzled. Then he suddenly leaped in alarm as Zack appeared beside him, hopped up and down and disappeared again. Now Max and Ben could see a very surprised crab being flung about in mid air, attached to the tail of the invisible Zack.

"What do you call a gargoyle with a crab hanging onto his tail?" shrieked Bart, slapping his gladiator skirt in delight.

"I don't know," chorused the others.

"Zack!" spluttered Bart. The gargoylz rolled about on the sand, holding their round bellies and chuckling at the flying crab.

"Stand still, Zack!" called Ben as the crab whipped past his face. "And make yourself visible. Then I can rescue you."

Pop! Zack came into view, shaking his tail with the crab still firmly attached. Ben grabbed hold of the end, gently removed the crab and put it safely in a nearby pool.

"Spluttering gutterz!" gasped Zack. "Ira was right. The seaside's dangerous."

"But it *was* funny," gurgled Toby. "I haven't laughed so much since Cyrus put everyone to sleep in the middle of the vicar's sermon."

"Teacher ahoy!" announced Ira suddenly.

Max looked up. Mr Widget was calling everyone over to the coach.

"Time to go home," sighed Ben.

The gargoylz looked crestfallen.

"You'd better get on board before the rest of us," Max told them.

"Aye, aye." Ira saluted before giving the order. "Form a line, shipmates."

Max and Ben gathered up their things and joined their class.

"Anyone seen Barry Price?" Mr Widget was asking anxiously.

"Help!" A distant cry echoed across the sand. "Get me out of here!"

"I think he's stuck, sir," said Ben.

Mr Widget raced over to where Barry was trapped. The Basher was complaining loudly.

"How did you manage to bury yourself in the sand?" they heard the teacher demanding as he tugged him out.

Max and Ben raced to the back of the coach. They could see a row of eyes under the seat. The engine started and very soon the boys could hear muffled gargoyle snoring.

"That was a great school trip!" said Max as the coach rumbled back towards Oldacre School.

"We've worn the gargoylz out," said Ben with a grin. "No need to keep them quiet this time."

"They didn't even need Cyrus's song to make them fall asleep," Max added with a smile.

"We're not *all* asleep," came a squawk. Ira popped his beak out and winked at the boys. "Someone has to make sure the ship gets safely back to harbour!"

Gargoylz Fact File

Full name: Tobias the Third
Known as: Toby
Special Power: Flying
Likes: All kinds of pranks and mischief – especially playing jokes on the vicar
Dislikes: Mrs Hogsbottom, garden gnomes

Full name: Barnabas
Known as: Barney
Special Power: Making big stinks!
Likes: Cookiez
Dislikes: Being surprised by humanz

Full name: Eli
Special Power: Turning into a grass snake
Likes: Sssports Day, Sssslithering
Dislikes: Ssscary ssstories

Full name: Bartholomew

Known as: Bart

Special Power: Burping spiders

Likes: Being grumpy

Dislikes: Being told to cheer up

Full name: Theophilus

Known as: Theo

Special Power: Turning into a ferocious tiger (well, tabby kitten!)

Likes: Sunny spots and cosy places

Dislikes: Rain

Full name: Zackary

Known as: Zack

Special Power: Making himself invisible to humanz

Likes: Bouncing around, eating bramblz, thistlz, and anything with pricklz!

Dislikes: Keeping still

Full name: Ira
Special Power: Making it rain
Likes: Making humans walk the plank
Dislikes: Being bored

Name: Azzan
Special Power: Breathing fire
Likes: Surprises
Dislikes: Smoke going up his nose and making him sneeze

Name: Cyrus
Special Power: Sings lullabies to send humanz to sleep
Likes: Fun days out
Dislikes: Snoring